HOOKERS & BLOWE

HOOKERS & BLOWE

Mhairi Simpson

www.skytintbooks.co.uk

Hookers & Blowe © Mhairi Simpson 2012

Cover art by Kevin Lester
Additional effects by Mhairi Simpson

ISBN-13: 978-1-910658-04-8
ISBN-10: 1910658-04-9

SkyTint Books
www.skytintbooks.co.uk
mhairi@skytintbooks.co.uk

Second edition
This edition published by SkyTint Books in 2014
This story was previously published by Anachron Press in 2012.

For Hamish, who keeps playing
Liz, who keeps picking up the phone
and Leona, without whom I'd have more time to
write the next one

Hookers & Blowe

8

Light floods into the cupboard as the door flies open, slamming against the wall. Robby Blowe jumps but doesn't make a sound. He watches a hand reach in and wrap tightly around his arm. It hurts.

It hurts more when the hand pulls him out, bending his arm in a way it doesn't want to bend. He hits his head on the inside of the cupboard as he slides out and he can't stop a whimper. It falls out of his mouth like a stone.

"You shouldn't hide from your daddy, Robby." Daddy's eyes look strange. Robby wonders if this is really his daddy, or if his real daddy died already and this... thing took over his body. It's wishful thinking. This is his real Daddy. He knows him too well.

Daddy stands up and Robby screams as his shoulder twists. He daren't look. He's scared his arm isn't there anymore. It hurts more than any other time. And Daddy is smiling. Robby turns cold all over, because he knows Daddy won't stop this time. Robby won't wake up in hospital. He won't wake up at all.

He starts to cry.

Daddy starts to tell him off, but his voice rises and keeps rising.

Now Daddy's screaming. His voice isn't strong or soft or serious anymore. It's shrill — a cut through Robby's head — and he slaps his hands over his ears. That's when he finds Daddy isn't holding his arm anymore.

Robby slides backwards, nearly screaming again when he tries to use his left arm. After that he only uses his right arm and his feet, pushing himself away from his daddy. He looks taller from down here on the floor, even screaming so loud that his face is red and his eyes are watering. Or is he crying? Robby can't tell. There's a bad smell, like burnt dinner, and it's making Robby's eyes water too.

Daddy's arms are outstretched, his fists clenched, and now it looks like his chest bulging. His screams get louder, impossibly louder, and Robby's hands can't block the sound out. But he can't shut his eyes either. He can't stop watching Daddy scream. And when he finally tears his eyes away, he sees something else.

Someone else.

A tall man, made of shifting shadows, stands at the other end of the kitchen. He holds a stick, a bar of shadow, in his hand, and there's a very thin line leading from the end of that shadow to Daddy's chest. It's a straight line, and it leads right to the centre of the bulge. Something sharp is poking out. Daddy's chest bulges more and more and his screams get louder and louder until a big fishhook pulls right out, taking a ball of light with it, and Daddy falls to the floor.

Robby watches the hook fly back to the shadow man. The man catches the ball of light, takes it off the hook, and puts it in a bag hanging from his waist. Then he looks at Robby.

Robby knows he mustn't scream, but as the shadow man moves closer, he can feel the fear rising in his throat. He's going to scream, he knows it. He's going to throw up, too.

The shadow man readies his hook and Robby whimpers, pushing himself backwards towards the cupboard. But he can't move fast enough. His arm hurts and he can't go fast enough to hide before the hook gets to

10

him. He looks over at his mother. She's staring at him, but not at him. It's like she's looking through him, like she doesn't see him at all. Tears burn behind his eyes. She's not going to help. But he won't look at the shadow man. Maybe if he doesn't look at him, he'll go away.

He screws his eyes up tight and remembers sitting in the garden with Mummy. They're eating squashed fly biscuits. Mummy tells him that everything has a spirit that lives on after it dies, and he makes his biscuits fly around because the spirits of the flies are still there, and Mummy laughs. It's a sunny day, warm and bright. If he concentrates really hard he can even feel the heat of the sun on his skin...

He opens his eyes. The shadow man is still there. But he's not moving any more. He's just looking at Robby. He seems confused. Then the hook comes flying towards Robby.

He throws up his hands and there's a flash of light and a very high scream, so high you can hardly hear it. Then the shadows just fade away.

Robby looks at Daddy. He's lying on the floor now. His mouth is still wide open. His eyes are showing white all around the coloured part. He looks like he's wearing a mask.

Robby slides back into the cupboard. Mummy is lying on the floor, too, and until she wakes up, the cupboard is the safest place to be.

And it doesn't smell as bad.

"Disturbance at 72 North Leas. Any units respond?"

The call made Detective Constable Robert Blowe sigh, but he stood up and headed for his car, ignoring the tiny man in brown and green who snuck out from behind the sugar bowl and tiptoed towards his barely touched coffee. He didn't know what it was, but he often saw it or something like it going for a half-finished coffee. It wasn't doing anyone any harm. Unlike bloody Johnny G.

He'd just come from bloody North Leas. The further his shift got past midnight, the better Sharon's coffee looked, but that was the downside of this job. People called in and cops responded. For all the good it did sometimes. Between the drugs and smacking his wife around, every cop in Fenton knew Johnny Grayson, of 72 North Leas, but they'd never been able to make charges stick.

There was already a marked car out front when Blowe arrived. The screaming was audible even with the window closed, but it was only when he opened his door that he realised there were two voices. One female. One male.

He burst into the house just ahead of the two constables from the marked unit who he vaguely recalled as Thorpe and Redd and barrelled through to the kitchen before skidding to a halt. He collided with the kitchen table before he could stop himself but barely noticed the impact. The room stank of burnt jam. Johnny Grayson was on the floor.

His wife, Carrie Grayson, was flat up against the cupboards in the opposite corner, hands braced against the workbench on either side, her mouth stretched too wide with her panicked cries. The screaming had made her face blotchy, an ugly mishmash of red, white and dark purple.

Johnny wasn't screaming, not any more. He lay full length on the floor, his face a mask of terror, eyes bulging, whites showing all around, and the dark pit of his mouth framed by yellow-white teeth. He looked like a grotesque parody of a corpse, even to Blowe who'd seen enough ugly deaths that one more should have been no surprise.

Eventually Blowe shook himself and waved a hand towards Carrie. Someone must have gone to her because her shrieks quickly faded to sobs. Blowe felt his head clear enough to approach the body. The smell wasn't as bad over here, which was strange because he was closer to the stove. Carrie did try, bless her. Not that anything was ever good enough for her piece of shit husband.

"Call it in," he said over his shoulder.

"Already done, sir."

At least someone was concentrating. Blowe shook his head. He was getting old.

He walked towards Johnny, taking it slow, just in case he'd missed something and the man wasn't as dead as he looked. He squatted down beside the body. Cold ran over his skin, making it prickle as every fine hair stood up.

Johnny G, drug-dealing scourge of North Leas, was dead alright, but there wasn't a mark on him.

Entering the station the next morning, Blowe fell into step beside DC Dale as they headed for the coffee-maker.

"Is it true about Johnny G dying of fear?" Dale asked as he poured a cup and handed it to Blowe.

"Looked that way," Blowe murmured, blowing on his coffee.

"What's wrong?"

"Nothing. It just..." Blowe trailed off, not sure what to say. "It's nothing."

He turned towards the stairs, but stopped as Dale caught his arm.

"It's never nothing with you. What's up?"

Blowe couldn't tell him. He just couldn't.

"I need to do some research," he said. "It seems similar to another case I remember hearing about, but I can't remember the details."

Dale snorted and let go of his arm.

"Enjoy your time in Database Hell."

Blowe grinned and lifted his coffee cup in farewell as he turned away.

He hated lying to Dale, the closest thing he had to a friend on the job, or anywhere, for that matter. But he couldn't be sure if he'd really seen what he thought he'd seen.

It was a long time ago, over thirty years now, and he'd only been a kid. As he sat down at his desk, the phone rang.

"Blowe."

"DC Madison from Fenton North. We've had a suspect inform us he knows something about the Killyben murders. Dispatch said it was your case. We thought you might like to come and observe the interview."

"Very kind of you. I'll be right over." Blowe put the phone down and downed his coffee in two gulps, gasping as it cauterised his throat. Research would have to wait. He tried not to think about whether he was pleased or disappointed. A lead on the Killyben murders was a good thing. He could be pleased about that, at least.

***

The suspect in North Fenton had a name or two that Blowe had to check out. One was nothing, the other, Jackson Lansdale, had vanished a couple of days previously and no one had seen him. Blowe took a detour on the way back to the station to knock on a few doors in North Leas, but no one had any information other than hearing a lot of screaming. They hadn't thought much of it because, y'know, it was the Graysons.

Yeah. Everyone knew Johnny Grayson. He shook his head as he entered the back of the station.

"Take your fuckin' 'ands off me, I never done nuffink!"

Blowe barely registered the commotion at the bottom of the stairs. Doyle Carmody was a toe rag, instigating all manner of idiocy and dragging his supposedly best mate, David Grace, down with him. Most of the station referred to them as Dingbat and Dormouse since Doyle obviously had no sense, and David never seemed to have an opinion on anything, just tagged along. It was a match made in Hell. David would end up in jail soon enough and he wouldn't do well inside. Doyle wouldn't go to jail, though. Doyle would be dead. His mouth was too big for him to survive much longer.

Blowe's head snapped up as he realised why Doyle's imminent death was a given, or had been. Doyle ran for Johnny G, or used to, and had started shooting his mouth off about setting up on his own. Blowe spun round and raced down the corridor in time to see the boys being hustled into separate interview rooms. A rumpled-looking man, all creases and bags under the eyes, was close behind. Blowe winced when he saw who it was, then steeled himself to shout.

"Jack!"

Sergeant Jack Dodson raised an eyebrow. Years back there'd been a disagreement involving three women and a lot of whisky. It had never really got sorted out, with the result that Dodson never spoke to Blowe if he could help it, and vice versa. Even Blowe knew he was breaking an unspoken rule by talking to Jack, but he couldn't let the opportunity slip.

"Not now," he said. "Those two , what are they in for?"

"Suspected of shoplifting. Witness reports matches Ding- Doyle, but David insisted on coming with. Why?"

"Ask both of them when they last saw Johnny G. He dropped dead last night. They might be able to shed some light on why, last movements, that kind of thing."

Jack's eyes brightened considerably.

"Do you think they might have…?"

Blowe snorted.

"I doubt it. Not exactly scary, are they? Whatever it was killed Johnny, he saw it coming, and it had him terrified." He thought it best not to mention the lack of obvious trauma. Poison required a level of sophistication Doyle could only hope to aspire to. "I just need to know if they saw anything."

Jack's face fell. No chance of a flashy murder conviction today. He nodded glumly and turned back to the interview room.

Blowe stood and watched him go. Then he headed for the mortuary.

Dr. Cameron was leaning over paperwork when he entered.

"I know you won't like me saying this, but it makes a change to be glad to see a person dead," she said as they headed over to the gurney holding Johnny's cadaver. "I've had to examine too many of his ex-clients."

Blowe grimaced and sighed.

"Any idea on the cause of death?"

"None whatsoever, I'm afraid. Looking at him, I'd say he was literally scared to death, which I didn't know was possible in one so young. It'll take a while for the blood tests to come back, but it'll most likely turn out to be heart failure brought on by drug abuse."

Blowe swallowed. He'd really hoped Cameron would find wounds or something, *anything,* to indicate a natural, or at least human, cause of death.

"Doesn't heart failure come on gradually? There are symptoms beforehand, right? I only ask because I spoke to him less than an hour before he died and he seemed in perfect health." *And as evil as ever.* "Besides, Johnny was one of the biggest, meanest bastards in Fenton. What would he be that afraid of? It doesn't make sense."

Cameron had no answer.

***

Blowe stood in the late Johnny G's kitchen, looking down at the floor where he'd last seen the man. It was spotless. Footsteps drew his attention to the living room and he headed on through to find a tech scanning the bookshelves with an ultraviolet light.

"Has someone cleaned the kitchen?"

"No, sir," the tech answered. "No one's been in there since the body was removed. It was already clean. We checked it and couldn't find anything out of place. So we're checking the rest of the house."

Blowe frowned.

"Nothing in there at all?"

She shook her head.

"Hair and fibres belonging to the wife and the deceased, and a couple of things we ruled out as belonging to you or the PCs. It's all been logged by Forensics."

"No… blood?"

"No, sir." The tech's voice was flat. She obviously didn't like having to repeat herself.

"The man was screaming loud enough to be heard from the street," Blowe pointed out. "I heard him before I opened my car door!"

"I know, sir, we were briefed. But there wasn't any blood. Just hair, fibres. A few footprints."

Blowe shook his head and gave in, then turned and stalked out of the house towards his car, muttering under his breath. A sharp breeze yanked at his coat, before softening to ruffle his hair. He slowed down as he neared the car, turning his head this way and that. He could almost smell something, something soft and homey.

He snorted. He hadn't smelt soft and homey in… ever.

"Good morning, Detective."

The voice was like a hammer wrapped in eastern velvet and it stopped him in his tracks. He turned to look at its owner, but it was like he was drowning in honey and it took forever to make eye contact. When he finally did, he only got a brief impression of golden skin framed with black hair which gleamed blue where the light hit it, and a flickering jewel set in the centre of her forehead, just below the hairline, before her eyes sucked him in.

Gold fringed in black, they drew him down a rollercoaster of red wine and maple syrup, landing him in a room with no door. Its stone walls were hung with metal tools, curved, thick, sharp. He'd never seen anything like them before, but electricity raced over his skin, sharp and bright, before melting to glorious heat which pooled in his groin. That part of his body knew what those were for, even if his brain didn't. They gleamed in the dancing light of a fire which burnt low in a deep fireplace. Opposite the fire was a huge bed, made with sheets that were black in the shadows, but a pure scarlet red where the light hit them.

Then he was standing on the pavement again, and a pair of scarlet red lips were moving, shaping words. He shook his head against a sudden wave of dizziness.

"What the-? Who are you?"

"Are you well, Detective?" The woman had a strange way of speaking, clipping her words off. English definitely wasn't her first language. Still, she sounded amused, rather than concerned.

He stared at her. Her lips were captivating. The colour, the way the curves flowed as she spoke…

"Detective? Oh, for blood's sake."

The scent, that warm scent of honey and vanilla vanished, leaving Blowe horribly aware of the cold breeze biting through his shirt and the faint suggestion of burnt meat in the air. And the fact he was staring at a total stranger.

"Yehgrh." He cleared his throat and tried again. "Yes. How can I help?"

She held out a hand.

"I am Suzanna. I'm pleased to meet you."

Blowe ignored the part of his brain that was agreeing most emphatically that he was also really, *really* pleased to meet her and shook her hand.

"Detective Robert Blowe. Pleased to meet you too."

"How is your day going, Detective?"

"Uh, it's, er, fine. It's going, um, well. I think. What was your name again?"

She smiled.

"How did the man die, Detective?"

For a moment Blowe couldn't think what she was talking about. Someone had died? You'd think he'd have noticed. Then he remembered and his face burned with embarrassment.

"Oh, he, er, well, I can't discuss the details of an ongoing case. Besides which, we don't actually know yet. We're waiting for the coroner's report." He fell back on the stock excuse with relief.

She put her head on one side, considering him like a dog considers a treat.

"You haven't seen anything like this before?"

"No," he said, frowning. Then his jaw dropped as he remembered a pillar of shadow in the corner of a room, a ball of light, and a man lying on the floor, apparently unharmed, but dead all the same. Fury coiled in the pit of his stomach. "How do you...?"

He stopped and stared.

She was gone.

***

Blowe stood outside number 72, staring at the house and shivering. Carrie had gone to stay with relatives, the next door neighbours told him. He was amazed she had any, but pleased. He doubted she'd ever return to this house. She hadn't had a happy life here.

He didn't know why he was back here. He told himself he wanted to talk to the neighbours, but junior officers had taken statements. He knew because he'd read them. No one saw anything. No one knew anything. Even Carrie hadn't seen anything, and she'd been standing right there. No doubt that was what had scared her so much, seeing Johnny apparently in agony, presumably under atttack, but no sign of an assailant.

He shook his head. It felt fluffy, like he was feeling his way around with none of his usual incisiveness. He suspected it had something to do with Suzanna. How had she known about the shadowy thing he saw as a child? He still wasn't entirely convinced that had been real, but Suzanna, a total stranger, had known.

Or had she? He thought back over the conversation, or tried to. It was rather hazy now. He remembered golden eyes and scarlet lips, and heat. His groin stirred in memory and he groaned, ashamed of his body's reaction while he was supposed to be on a murder case.

But was it even a murder case? There was nothing to say Johnny had actually been murdered. There was certainly no evidence to suggest he had been. Just a hunch. Blowe was used to his hunches. They'd never lied to him yet. But sometimes there was just no way to act on them, not legally, and this looked like it might be one of those times.

All things considered, he'd really rather Johnny had dropped dead of a heart attack, but it was looking less and less likely.

Being a cop meant you didn't always get to choose what did and didn't happen to you, what you did and didn't see. In fact, you almost never did.

The sun was low enough now that it was forced to slip between buildings, and could only cast the occasional strip of golden light across the road and pavements. The air was cooling and Blowe had his head down as he forced himself down the road. Then he heard it, the thin, pinprick yell of a human in fear of its life.

Not again, he thought, but he was in the nearest alleyway before he'd completed the thought. He barely slowed as he turned a corner, with the result that he ricocheted off the opposite wall and grunted as the air was forced from his lungs. He didn't take time to recover, though, staggering on as he gasped for breath, following the wails of terror down a slit between two buildings.

Not quite managing to turn the next corner, he slammed into solid brick and had to shake the stars from his vision before he could see clearly again. Then nausea threatened as he registered another body, crumpled where the wall met the tarmac. A few feet away, beyond the corpse, stood a pillar of shadow, shaped like a man, carefully reeling in a dark, blurring rod and reaching for the ball of light fizzing around the hook at the end of the line. Blowe recoiled, gasping, as the stench of burnt meat hit him, bringing tears to his eyes, and the shadow man looked up and saw him. Blowe clapped his arm over his mouth and nose, realising this was what he'd smelled in the Graysons' kitchen, and wondering if the creature was solid enough to handcuff.

"You," the thing breathed in a voice like the wind through a graveyard. "You were supposed to die."

Blowe blinked and shifted closer, unable to break the habit of checking a victim's pulse even though he knew this one had to be dead. No one looked like that while they were alive.

"I was?" He croaked the words, then coughed. He couldn't think of a single time his life had been in danger. Unless you counted that night when he was six... Oh god. "That was you?"

"No!" The creature looked down at the bag. "Twenty-one," it murmured, regretfully. "No room for yours."

It turned and began to glide away, and Blowe staggered after it.

"Wait!" Then he wanted to slap himself. He pulled himself together and sprinted down the alleyway, gathering himself and leaping at the man made of shadows.

He fell right through him, a wash of cold, acrid air enveloping him so that he couldn't breathe, and then releasing him in time to hit the pavement. Hard.

A dry, dry chuckle floated around him and he turned over, groaning, to see the dark above and before him roiling in patterns that turned his stomach.

"You cannot arrest me, Detective. But feel free to try. I will keep my bag free for you and your army."

"My army?"

"Indeed. All those many, many humans who believe in demons. I'm sure they will follow you to their deaths. And yours."

The shadows lightened and the acrid scent faded away.

Blowe gasped in lungfuls of clean air and wished, through the pounding in his head, that he hadn't done something so stupid. When he could breathe without wanting to throw up, he turned back to the body, pulling his mobile phone out of his jacket pocket. An army. Right. Like anyone would believe in something they couldn't see.

***

Blowe glared at his computer. The scene had been utterly clear of evidence, as he'd known it would be. Something made of shadow wasn't going to leave hair or skin or fibres behind, was it? He had wondered if the light would leave some kind of trace, but obviously not. Or not that modern, real world forensics could pick up, anyway.

He didn't know for sure, but he suspected he knew what was being taken.

Souls. It was stealing people's souls.

While they were still alive.

Jackson Lansdale shouldn't even have been in this area, and Blowe was now doubly pissed off. Not only was this... thing... killing people on his patch, it had also taken out a key lead in another case. It appeared to know Blowe, and that was disturbing enough, but to start messing with Blowe's job was unforgiveable.

He had to do something, but he had no idea what, and no evidence meant no case. His only window was from now until the coroner's report, which would no doubt say the death was unexplained and leave it at that. He had to move fast, but who could he talk to about this? Besides, apart from all that, how did you arrest something you couldn't even touch?

***

Blowe's desk trembled as he slammed his hands down on it. For thirty-two years he'd managed to convince himself that he'd more or less hallucinated the night his father died, but he couldn't ignore the similarities between his father's death and Johnny G's. And now the memory had broken free and he couldn't forget the fear he'd felt. He might have been surprised not to have made the connection sooner, but he'd only been six at the time, and who wanted to remember how their parents died? He knew what had killed his mother, and that was bad enough. At least his father was human. Technically.

He'd got used to seeing odd things over the years. He'd done his best to forget that experience at the age of six, but that hadn't been the first, nor the last. After that, though, he'd known what to be scared of. So seeing a tiny man appear in front of him in a crowded shopping centre, look very confused, and disappear again wasn't a problem. Nor was seeing the odd firefly that was too big to be a firefly, and had feet and a conical hat.

Once he was old enough to wander around the local library on his own, he'd started reading, and then the internet had opened up a whole universe of information that hadn't previously been available to him. So he knew Suzanna was most likely a succubus and best given a wide berth. Which was fine as long as she didn't come near him again. No man was a match for a succubus. He just had to hope whatever had prevented her from draining him of life would continue to be the case.

In all his research, though, he'd very rarely come across something like the shadow man and he'd never found any information on how to kill/vanquish/exorcise it. So he still didn't know why it hadn't been able to hook him when he was six and he had no idea at all who to ask. Any way he played it out in his head ended with him in a psychiatric wing, and he'd be useless to anyone locked up.

He was glad Johnny was dead. He was glad his father was dead, too. But what if this thing killed again? Would it only kill bad people? Was it okay to turn a blind eye to that? Maybe the best option was just to hope it didn't kill again. After all, as far as he knew, it had been thirty-two years between kills. He sighed. He wished he felt confident that it really had been that long, and this killer would now go away for the same amount of time. He might have been able to live with that kind of interval.

But he'd read Carrie Grayson's statement. She was a qualified nurse and adamant something had killed her husband, something other than natural causes. Which meant she expected the police to do something about it.

Blowe sighed again.

***

The park wasn't doing its job today. It hadn't for a while now, if he were honest with himself. For years, when things weren't making sense, when a con got away because of a legal loophole or the system sent an innocent down, he'd come here and sit for a while. Feel the breeze on his face, listen to it play with the leaves in the trees, see the grass and plants dance in the sunlight. Or the rain. Either way, the wildlife here thrived. Birds and squirrels, even rabbits. Whatever the weather, whatever the circumstances, every year there were baby birds cheeping in new nests, and no doubt more young things hidden away underground or in the trunks of various trees. It reminded him that things generally worked out for the best. With that clarity generally came inspiration, perspective.

Well, that was the idea.

It hadn't worked for a while, though. Not since Sherry… He shook away that line of thought. It didn't lead anywhere good. Experience had made that clear. He wrinkled his nose as an acrid scent wafted past, and then looked around sharply for shadows with short, blurred fishing rods. Instead he saw a group of young things, probably from the university, having a barbecue. He looked away as they started throwing a frisbee around. So young. So unaware of all the shit waiting for them in the world. Staring down at his hands, he wondered if he was going to end up in an asylum, going crazy every time someone walked past with sausages or an overcooked steak. At the very least this business threatened to make him too cynical to help the world. And that was why he'd become a cop, or he thought it was. To help people. To protect them. How was he going to protect them against this creature?

"Good afternoon, Detective."

The words impacted just before Suzanna's familiar, rich scent overrode his brain. But as quickly as the pit opened up in front of him, it closed again, leaving him bemused and staring at the woman from that morning.

"I see I will have to be careful around you, Detective. You are very sensitive."

"Really?"

She sat down beside him and crossed her legs. Blowe averted his eyes.

"And you are aware of your weaknesses. I admire that in a man."

"What can I do for you, miss, er…?"

"Forgotten so soon. You wound me, Detective."

He turned his head to look at her and immediately regretted it. He'd thought he'd misremembered the colour of her eyes.

He hadn't.

"You are preoccupied, Detective. Maybe I shall leave you to your thoughts." She stood, and he reached out and grabbed her, without really knowing why. She stared down at his hand gripping her wrist, and he found his hold loosening against his will.

"What do you want from me?" His throat was dry. He started to clear it, then she put her hand on his thigh and he forgot what he'd been doing.

"Nothing at all, Detective. I am curious about you, but I am sure time will tell me more."

"What? So... why are you talking to me?" Blowe was confused, and more than a little ashamed. He didn't want her

26

to go, and he had no rights to her time, or anyone else's. He had a problem that he needed to solve.

She considered him for a moment before answering.

"I merely wanted to talk to you. Do people not do this?"

Blowe stared at her. Beautiful women weren't in the habit of appearing at his side, intent on holding a conversation about nothing in particular. He could imagine Sherry making flapping motions with her hands and stage-whispering at him to get to it.

"Er, yes. I suppose they do. What would you like to talk about?"

"You, Detective. I am very curious about you."

Blowe frowned at her.

"Look, miss, I'm…" He swallowed. How did anyone get lips that red without lipstick?

"Detective, I mean no disrespect. I am simply… Okay, I will be honest with you. I need help. Your help. Please?" She laid a hand on his knee and he stared at it. How had that happened?

Help. She wanted his help. His head cleared instantly. This he could deal with.

"What happened?"

"My friend saw her husband die." She leaned forward, her dark eyes serious. "He screamed and screamed as thought in terrible pain, but there were no marks on him. The police will not investigate because of 'lack of evidence'." She spat the words out.

"Well." It came out as 'erhr' and he cleared his throat and started again. "I'm a cop. As you know. Have been for years. But I'm not sure I can help you…"

"Please, Detective, let me tell you the story."

The sun was low when he finally looked away from those cherry red lips. The barbecuers were still there, but the air was fresh and clear. Light filtered between buildings in distinct shafts, like God's fingers were brushing the trees of the park, gilding them and the grass beneath. The late afternoon sunlight touched the woman's face, too. He hadn't thought she could look any more beautiful.

"I wish I could help," he said.

Her smile widened into something toothy and genuine.

"I know," she told him.

And then she walked away.

"Wait!"

She turned around, eyebrows lifted.

"Are you following me?"

"Yes."

"Why?"

She considered him for a moment, or maybe she was just considering her response. The breeze strengthened, and for a single moment, the honey and vanilla scent cleared entirely.

"You are important," she said.

This time, when she walked away, she kept going. And Blowe realised the park had done its job after all. His head was clear, and he knew what he needed to do next.

"When in doubt, ask a snout," he muttered to himself as he left the park.

***

He paused on the pavement and looked towards the next corner. He rolled his eyes and headed that way. You got nothing unless you asked. Although in this case asking might get him a padded cell rather than information.

Digger was thin the way only long time users were thin. Blowe watched him shiver on a street corner, glancing in every direction in that awkward chicken-headed way that screamed "I'm about to meet the cop I'm informing" and wondered how he'd survived this long. He looked like a stiff breeze would bowl him over. And that didn't encourage longevity on the streets.

"Digger," he said quietly, pausing on the kerb as though to cross the road.

"Detective." Digger was a grave, well-educated man, and contrary to his appearance he was neither an addict, nor homeless. Blowe had never succeeded in figuring exactly who Digger was. He didn't show up in any records.

"Chat?" Blowe didn't know what Digger did and he was happy to keep it that way, as Digger seemed happy like that and no one knew more about what went on in this city than Digger. More to the point, no one knew Blowe better than Digger. He was the only one who knew about the things Blowe saw, and he knew they weren't hallucinations, because he saw them too.

Digger didn't reply, merely turned and walked away. Blowe looked both ways at the traffic sweeping along both sides of the road and shook his head in apparent defeat, turning to follow his contact a moment later.

He took his time, he had access to a car and Digger would have to take the bus, but when he finally pushed the diner's door open, Digger was already seated at a booth in the back, facing away from the door. He ordered a couple of coffees and then joined his friend. Colleague. Something like that, anyway.

"Two bodies in two days, Detective. That's impressive, even for you."

Blowe sighed.

"I'd rather get the guy behind the deaths than the bodies."

Digger put his head on one side.

"I thought their hearts stopped. Just dropped dead, they say."

Their eyes met.

"That's what the coroner says," Blowe hedged. "It's a bit…"

"Untidy?"

Blowe grinned in spite of himself.

"I was going to say coincidental. Sudden Death Syndrome isn't restricted to babies, but two sudden deaths, for no apparent reason, in two days?" He rolled his shoulders. It rankled that he knew who, or rather what, was responsible and couldn't work out what to do about it.

"You can't solve them all, Detective."

"I know." Blowe sighed heavily. "I know. It just…"

He trailed off and now it was Digger's turn to sigh. He leaned forward.

"Stay out of this one, Detective. There's nothing for you there."

"You know, you're the second person to tell me that. I can't leave it. You know that. Digger?"

Digger's face was a mask, blank, with something dark and sharp twisting behind his eyes. Silence drew out, wrapped around them, creating a bubble where it was just them. Them and a spark, one of those lines of knowledge that spring up over the course of a long friendship. Or partnership. Or something in between.

"You can't arrest it, that's for sure. Look, they were both dealers. Could have been any number of things that took them down."

"But it wasn't, was it? It was one thing — one thing that took both of them down. Hooked them and ripped their—" Blowe broke off, realising Digger was staring at him. "I'm sorry. I… I'm sorry."

"You saw it," Digger murmured.

"Yeah. Well, no. I only got there after it was over."

"No." Digger's hands spread over the table. "You saw *it*."

Blowe frowned, then realised what he meant.

"You knew," he whispered, partly grateful he wasn't the only one, and partly horrified that the only person he could confide in about these things had come so close to death. Because surely to see one was to risk being killed by it. "You've seen it too?"

"Once," said Digger. "That was enough."

Blowe thought back, back to a kitchen and the thud of fist on flesh, and a small, dark cupboard. And screams. Digger was right. Once would have been enough. But he'd heard those screams three times now. Some things couldn't be wiped from your mind. Not ever.

"What is it?" he asked.

Digger sipped his coffee before answering.

"I don't know any true names, but they're known as Hookers."

"There's more than one?" Blowe was aghast. One was bad enough. But in a group? "How do I stop it?"

Digger's eyes opened wide.

"Stop it? You don't. No one does. Don't you know what it is?"

Blowe looked blank.

"It's a demon, man! You can't arrest it! And even if you did, there'd be another one along sooner or later. Most people can't even see them. You can't exactly get the DI to mount an operation. He wouldn't even approve of you opening a case!" He shook his head and lifted his coffee cup to take a sip. The cup wobbled against his lips, a silent testament to his shaking hands. "Just stay out of their way. Stay away from them and move on with your life."

"I can't do that. They're killing people."

"You did get the bit about demons, right? It's kind of implied in the name."

"Right. Demons." Blowe jabbed his thumb into his own chest. "Copper. Protects the citizens — even the scumbag drug dealers. I can't let it go."

"Then you'll be next. It's been nice knowing you." Digger drained his cup and left.

Blowe sat there for a long time after Digger went. Curiously, it wasn't the thought of dying that bothered him. It was the thought that if he died, he wouldn't be able to stop these bastard demons from killing anyone else. Jackson had been a small-timer. He could have been saved. From the drugs. Not from the demon, though. Blowe hadn't been able to save him from that.

Demons.

Good thing he'd decided for sure, a long time ago, that he wasn't mad. This might have made him think again. He drained his cup and stood, and wasn't nearly as surprised as he should have been to find Digger standing beside the bench.

"You won't leave it, will you." It wasn't a question.

Blowe shook his head.

Digger let out a breath.

"There is something. Maybe," he added as Blowe smiled. "No guarantees. It's picky about who it works for."

Blowe frowned.

"Who what works for?"

But his contact was already leading the way out of the diner.

Digger led him to a small shop tucked away in the maze of alleyways between what used to be Johnny G's street and the river. The door boasted no less than four keyholes, but

Digger didn't need a key. He laid a palm against the door and muttered something too low for Blowe to hear. Locks slid and clicked and the door opened.

The shop was dimly lit and seemed small, but as Blowe's eyes adjusted to the light, he realised it was bigger than he'd thought. It was just that it was so full it seemed smaller.

Blowe couldn't see the walls, and he wasn't even sure where they were, as they were hidden by boxes, small and large, piled up in groups, statues and statuettes, wooden and glass cases, and shelves, which he was fairly sure stood against the walls. He couldn't be certain, though, as they were jammed full of ornaments, boxes, curious arrangements of metal and stone and a number of things he couldn't see properly. There were paths through the shop, between piles of... things, and Blowe found himself regretting his height as his head connected with more unidentifiable objects hanging from the ceiling.

Digger led the way, Blowe trying to keep one eye on him and one on the various pieces strewn around. The dim light played tricks on his eyes and he couldn't tell what was moving and what wasn't. Technically, of course, everything should have been still, but he kept seeing things out of the corner of his eye, things that didn't make sense unless you had experience of stuff moving when it shouldn't.

A bead curtain rattled in front of him and he faced forward in time to get smacked in the face by lines of wooden beads handing from the ceiling. He pushed them aside and stepped through to find Digger standing in front of a rare clear spot against the wall of the shop. Blowe frowned and looked around. Every other wall was covered, utterly hidden from floor to ceiling. Except for this six foot space. Clear from the floor to the wall mount holding a long straight sword, and clear above and for three or four feet to either side, too. He looked at Digger, eyebrows raised in question. Digger looked embarrassed.

"It likes its space," he said out of the corner of his mouth.

Blowe looked up at the sword.

"Uh..."

Digger shushed him.

"Be very careful what you say next."

Blowe thought about it, then closed his mouth. After a few more moments' silence, he ventured a question.

"Are we just going to look at it?"

Digger glared at him.

"You have no idea what you're looking at, do you?" he snapped.

There didn't seem to be a good response to this.

Digger sighed.

"It's a weapon, which you might, *might*, be able to use against the Hookers. But, like I said, it's very particular. Not everyone can wield it. In fact, most people can't. And I don't know if you can."

"What's the worst that can happen?"

Digger didn't reply.

"As bad as that, eh?" Blowe looked up at the weapon. It was about as long as his arm with a cold steel look that spoke of sharpness and practical killing. "Only one way to find out, right?"

He didn't say anything when Digger took a step back, then another. Just reached out and laid one finger very gently on the hilt.

The effect was instanteous. One moment he was standing in Digger's shop, the next he was on a hilltop, looking up at a man hanging from a cross. The victim's eyes, slitted against the sun and the pain, gleamed through the

34

blood that had run down his face from the thorns on his head. Blowe wanted to look away and couldn't. He could only watch as his arm rose and plunged a spear into the man's side.

He blinked, unable to see for a moment in the dimly lit room. Very carefully, he lifted his finger off the hilt of the sword.

"Rob?"

"I'm fine," he whispered, although he wasn't sure if he was. "What. Is. That?"

Digger reached out and took the sword down.

"Oh, so you can touch it?" Blowe felt somehow cheated.

"Of course I can touch it. I just didn't want to be touching it if it rejected you." Digger turned the sword over in his hands, then slid the blade clear of the scabbard. "Have you heard of the Spear of Destiny?"

Blowe frowned.

"Yeah. It's the spear the Roman soldier used to pierce..." He trailed off, his gaze flickering from Digger's face to the sword and back. "But that was a spear."

"It looked like a spear. Probably because the soldier was most used to handling spears. Most often it looks like this, but... Here." He held it out and Blowe automatically recoiled. "Take it, man, it won't hurt you. Otherwise you wouldn't still be standing here."

Blowe reached out and gingerly took the sword from Blowe's hands.

"Yeah? Where would I - what the fuck?"

There was no flashy display of lights, no rush of heat or tingling. The sword merely... changed. In the time it took him to wrap his hand around the hilt and lift it clear of Digger's hands, it had lost its long, flat, sword-like appearance. In its place lay a 9mm Glock handgun.

"I hate to repeat myself, but what... What is this?"

"It's whatever you need it to be," Digger told him quietly.

"But what-"

"That's the best I can do, Rob. Honestly, I don't know any more than that."

Blowe lifted the gun, examining it from all angles before he thought to check the safety. It was on. He ejected the magazine and thumbed a round into his palm. It was a dark, coppery red.

"Red?" As soon as the word left his mouth, he wished he hadn't asked. Digger didn't reply, and Blowe was glad. He replaced the round, and loaded the magazine back into the gun. Then he checked the safety again. Just in case.

"It'll never misfire."

"What?" Blowe had been examining some script apparently etched into the barrel and now he looked up. "What was that?"

"The gun." Digger nodded at the weapon. "It'll never misfire. It'll never jam. And it'll never go off by accident."

"Oh. Great."

"And it'll never miss. So be bloody careful what you aim at."

Blowe stared at him, then ejected the magazine and did a thirty-odd point check to make absolutely sure there wasn't a round left in the barrel. He put the magazine in one pocket, then stood looking at his inside jacket pocket. He couldn't put a handgun in there. Apart from it being illegal to carry handguns in the UK anyway, he just didn't feel right doing it.

"There'll be a holster," Digger said.

"A what?"

In response, Digger reached past the hand holding his jacket out so he could see the front pocket and pulled something forward into Blowe's line of sight. Sure enough, it was a leather holster. Now he knew it was there, he could feel it around his shoulders, a very slight, but barely there, constriction as he moved his arms.

"Digger," he began but Digger shook his head.

"You need this, Rob. There's no other way."

The gun slid into the holster and he barely felt it beneath his jacket as he left the shop. All the same, he couldn't get the image of those copper red bullets out of his mind.

***

Logically Blowe knew the station looked exactly the same as it had when he'd left that morning, but he found himself staring hard at any shadows, trying to discern shapes in them. Humanoid shapes. Faces. Sticks. Fishhooks. And all the while he could feel the comforting weight of the gun against his chest.

He sat down at his desk and tried to focus. There wasn't much point in writing up a report on the body he'd found that morning. As far as pretty much everyone was concerned, it was just another body. Just another death in the Maze. Another dealer died. The reasons didn't really matter. A criminal died? What a pity.

But it mattered to Blowe. Always had. That was why he'd become a copper in the first place. To protect those who couldn't protect themselves. Even if usually they were the biggest baddest son-of-a-bitch on the block. If they went down, it was his job to take up the slack, to find who did it, to get justice for the wronged.

Because murder was wrong, and that was that. Some people, quite a few coppers among them, had a bit of a moral grey area here. Most of the people in the precinct thought Johnny G dropping dead was a gift from above. Blowe didn't. Blowe called it murder, and murder was a crime.

The keyboard clicked beneath his fingers and he watched the screen as he put search terms into the database. Names and dates filled the screen and he started reading.

There were a lot more unexplained deaths in the database than he would have liked to see, but he wasn't surprised. It was amazing how, even with the advancements made by modern science, so many deaths still defied explanation. Although, given what he'd seen today, he was starting to wonder if more of those deaths could have been explained by something other than modern science.

A lot of the names were familiar: men and women he'd arrested at various points over the years. When you'd been on the force long enough, even in a small city like Fenton, eventually you got to know who was who. The criminal community, like most professional communities, was a small, incestuous one. Between his arrest record, those of his colleagues, and contacts like Digger —though none as comprehensive as he — Blowe knew a lot of criminals.

But a lot of the names weren't familiar, and when he went into those files, they often turned out not to be criminals. The unexplained deaths had no pattern. The demons didn't just kill bad people, or even stupid people who did bad things. They killed anyone who got in their way.

More than three quarters of the deaths occurred in bad areas, usually late at night, sometimes early in the morning. Many of the rest were paired with the death of a criminal, usually a petty thief, sometimes a B&E specialist. Wallets from one were often found on the other. It didn't take him long to put a scenario together.

Petty criminal mugs some unsuspecting passer-by. Demon shows up, hooks thief. Unsuspecting passer-by tries to help and gets killed as well?

Blowe shook his head. Why would they attack innocents? Then he remembered the shadow in the alley. They'd attack anyone. They didn't care. They just wanted the souls.

How was he going to protect anyone, least of all himself, against something like that?

A *click* made him look down. The Glock of Destiny lay on his desk, with Blowe's hand around the grip. He didn't even remember taking it out of the holster.

"Alright," he said, after a quick glance around the office to make sure he was alone. "You're thousands of years old and you've got a mind of your own. I get it. But I'm a cop. A police officer. I uphold the law! I can't go around shooting peop— things. Even if no one else can see them. *Especially* if no one else can see them. I'll be in a hospital for the criminally insane before you say "demonic soul fisherman"."

Blowe was almost surprised when the gun didn't talk back, and he realised with annoyance that he was disappointed. He wanted a gun to solve his problems for him?

"Ugh," he grunted. "We know that doesn't solve anything."

He slid the weapon back into the shoulder holster and headed for the door.

He was heading back out onto the street when he ran into DI McDonald coming the other way around a corner.

"How's it going, Blowe? What are you working on?"

Blowe considered the DI carefully. His eyes seemed a little sharp for this time of night.

"Just checking out some stats, sir. There have been a lot of unexplained deaths."

"Not recently."

"Two, in two days. But I was actually referring to all the others."

The DI looked around, grabbed Blowe's arm, and hustled him into his office. He shut the door, then went and sat behind his desk.

"What are you talking about?"

"Three hundred and forty-six unexplained deaths in the last two years. Several thousand if you go back far enough. That's a lot of unexplained deaths, sir."

They sat there in silence for a minute. The DI finally spoke.

"So some criminals bought it for no apparent reason. Are we really going to cry over them?"

"If it was just criminals, probably not, although if someone was killing them off we'd call them vigilantes and that's illegal too."

Colson smiled and made to stand.

"But it's not just criminals."

Colson's smile vanished.

"It's innocent civilians too. Sometimes it looks like whoever, or whatever, killed the criminal did so immediately after they'd robbed a civilian, and then the civilian died too. That's a vigilante getting trigger-happy, and it's not right. Two people dropping dead for no reason in two days is bad enough, but two people dropping dead within minutes, and feet, of each other? Sir, that's more than happenstance. More than coincidence, even."

"You think it's enemy action?"

Blowe wanted to smile, to relax into a decades-old friendship. Their mutual love of James Bond (the books, not the films) was something Colson and Blowe had bonded over during training. But that was a long time ago now. He swallowed. Was he really going to go through with this?

"It has to be, sir." If in doubt, hedge. "There's no other explanation."

Colson's fingers drummed a staccato beat on his desk.

"Look, Blowe, you've been very busy lately. When was the last time you took some holiday? You've got plenty owing. Take a few weeks off, get refreshed, then come back and I'm sure this will all make more sense."

"I can't do that, sir. Someone's killing people. A lot of people. I want to investigate."

The DI's hands slammed down on the surface of his desk. Blowe flinched.

"These people are scumbags. Is it really so bad if they die?"

Blowe was shocked into silence.

"So some innocents get caught up in it from time to time. It's a small price to pay to clear the streets of the dross."

The silence was dark and deep. Blowe could hear his own heartbeat through the pounding of his pulse in his ears.

"You knew." It wasn't a question. The DI had already realised what he'd said, and his face was set in stubborn lines. He didn't regret a thing. "You knew and you let it happen."

"There is no 'letting' it happen, Detective Blowe. You've seen what it does. What do you think any of us could do against that? Just keep your head down and walk away. Otherwise you'll be next and there's nothing any of us can do to stop it."

Blowe knew his mouth was hanging open, but he couldn't muster up the will to close it. His DI, a man he'd looked up to throughout his career, was telling him to walk away from a murderer. And then he cast his mind back to the last time he'd brought in a career murderer. A hit man. His little black book had been full of details of the great and good up and down the country who had paid him to 'solve a problem' for them. With a bullet, or a knife, or some craftily administered poison. He'd killed so many people he would have been a perfect candidate for the death penalty, particularly as he showed no remorse whatsoever.

But instead of going to prison, he'd gone into Witness Protection, because he'd known people the police wanted more.

That was the day Blowe realised he would never make a real difference in the world. And now he realised he couldn't even keep trying anymore. There just wasn't any point.

"I'm sorry, sir. It's been a pleasure working with you."

"What?"

"You'll have my letter of resignation on your desk in the morning."

"Rob—!"

Blowe closed the door behind him and looked up and down the empty corridor, before heading back to his desk to write a letter.

***

The warmth of the day was long gone by the time he emerged from the station, his hair standing on end from his fingers running through it so often over the last few hours. He pulled his coat firmly around him and walked towards his car.

"Good evening, Detective."

The tantalising scents of honey and vanilla swirled around him and he staggered as his balance faded. He caught himself and turned around.

Suzanna seemed to glow in the street lights, but it was a dark sheen, an aura of danger and desire which made him sway towards her.

"Finished with work?" she asked, her voice curling around the nape of his neck, making his skin prickle as the tiny hairs rose and heat raced south. The jewel glittered above her eyes.

"Y-yes," he stuttered.

"Where are you going?"

"I, uh, I'm… I don't know."

"You look like you've had a hard day."

The reality of the last twenty-four hours cut through the haze and his shoulders dropped.

"You have no idea."

A frown flashed across her face, and then her features were clear and calm once more.

"Why don't we go for a drink, and you can tell me all about it?" Somehow she had reached him, or he had reached her, he didn't remember. But her arm was tucked under his, and they were walking up the street towards the lights of Seventeen Street. "I drink red wine."

He wasn't surprised.

She wanted to hear about him, and so he told her. When he got to the part about not wanting to be a cop anymore, she relaxed and her smile grew wider. His shaft followed suit, thickening between his legs. He wanted to know why such a woman was so interested in him, but she seemed enraptured, her eyes only on him, drinking him in, and he couldn't muster the energy to question why. If he'd been being honest with himself, he might have admitted he didn't want the fantasy to end. Part of him was quite certain he was dreaming all of this and he didn't want to wake up. Part of him was tired, and part of him didn't care. Nothing mattered except those ruby lips and golden eyes and that amazing perfume which constantly teased at his senses.

"Would you like a coffee?" Suzanna asked, and it was only then that Blowe realised he was a bit cold, and rather stiff, and his throat hurt.

"That would be lovely," he said, and she smiled and held out her hand. It seemed like an invitation to something else, but it was only coffee, right? Coffee with honey and vanilla, he hoped. What a wonderful combination that would be.

They were halfway down the street when a scream split the air.

Blowe stopped in his tracks, staring at the street around him, then at Suzanna.

"Where are we going?" he asked.

She stared at him, opened her mouth to reply, but her voice was drowned out by another scream.

Blowe was already running.

No maze of back alleys this time. Right around the next corner, Doyle Carmody was pressed up against a wall, clawing at his chest as the Hooker smiled and turned the reel on his rod. Blowe leapt forward, his hands closing around the hook to try and pull it out. If he could get it out before it hooked on to Doyle's soul, Doyle would be okay. He was a drain on society and probably better off dead, but not like this.

Blowe heaved and Doyle's screams redoubled.

"No!" Blowe yelled. It couldn't be too late. He had to be in time. This was his job, saving people's lives. Then he shrieked as cold burned through his palms, so deep and sharp he wondered if he'd be left with stumps. He didn't let go, though, even as he saw smoke rise. Doyle's voice weakened. Maybe he wasn't too late...

The hook shot free, a brilliant effervescent comet flying clear and straight to the Hooker's hand. Doyle dropped to the ground, his face frozen agape, his eyes wide with the agony he'd felt. Blowe collapsed, gasping for air, his hands forgotten.

"You bastard," he panted. "You fucking bastard."

The Hooker only grinned and dropped the soul in the bag, then looked at Blowe, reeled in the hook and prepared to cast again.

It was the faint scrabbling sound that alerted Blowe to the fact he wasn't actually the target. He turned to see David cowering behind some bins. He didn't waste time turning again to see what the Hooker was doing. He just grabbed the boy, hauled him to his feet and shoved him towards the corner. Suzanna was there, watching, shaking her head. She looked confused but he barely had time to wonder when she'd arrived, or how she'd kept up with him in those heels. He grabbed her, pretending he was helping her escape rather than to hold himself up.

"Run!" Then he pushed her forwards too, but she didn't move. "Oh crap. Look, you can't see it, but something really really bad is headed this way and we need to go now. Now!"

She gave him a pitying look. He threw back his head and grimaced at the sky. Then nearly fell over as she stepped forward. Towards the Hooker.

"No!" He spun around and grabbed for the nearest lamppost as his head threatened to lift off into space. He missed.

"Oof." From his position on the pavement, he saw Suzanna head towards the shadows. The Hooker smiled and raised his rod.

"No!"

The Hooker's shadowy face faltered. Suzanna's perfume swirled and the shadows paled. Was Blowe imagining this? Were they really becoming thinner? Less substantial? Less... there?

Blowe scrabbled under his jacket, biting back a yell of pain as fabric brushed the burns on his hands.

"Do not meddle, slut." The graveyard breeze voice sounded less sure than when it spoke to Blowe. More air, less substance. Not as cold or dry. It sounded almost human.

"I would not meddle. But you already found your prey. Leave. Hunt another." Suzanna's voice, on the other hand, was very different. Gone were the sultry tones that had held Blowe entranced every time they'd spoken. Here was steel and oak and blood, and weird harmonics that made the back of his neck prickle.

The Glock's grip was warm, warmer than he'd expected it to be, even though it had sat against his chest all day. He braced himself to close his wretched hand around the metal. It had to be done, no matter how much it hurt.

"You would put yourself in a Hell hunt?" The Hooker's voice bubbled with fury, but he didn't move forward.

"Find another. This one…" She paused. When she spoke again, Blowe could hear the smile in her voice. "Is mine."

It didn't hurt. The metal of the gun didn't hurt his hand. In fact, it soothed it, and he gripped it tighter, drawing it out of the holster.

"You—"

"Don't push me, Hell-spawn." Her voice snapped like a crocodile at the hooves of its prey. She looked more like a shadow than the Hooker, like a hole cut out of the world. So dark even the light didn't touch her. "You know I am not such easy prey as these. Hunt. Another."

Could he do it? Could he pull the trigger? He looked down the barrel at the creature of smoke and shadow and fiery hell.

"Hey, Hooker," he said, his voice a shred of its former self.

Both creatures turned to look at him. One a pillar of evil. He didn't know what Suzanna was. She sure as hell wasn't human, but for now she was on his side. The Hooker smiled, something gleaming in what passed for its mouth.

"You think to shoot me with a mortal weapon. Hahahaha." Its laugh was like autumn leaves crunching underfoot. It raised its arms and faced him. "Take your best shot."

"Detective," Suzanna looked nervous. "I'm not sure that's—"

The shot was horrendously loud, far louder than Blowe had anticipated. He saw the flame shoot from the end of the barrel, just like on the handguns he'd fired on the police range.

What he hadn't expected was the trail of light, red and gold and lilac, streaming from the end of the barrel straight into the Hooker. Nor did he expect the the thin, high-pitched scree of sound as the light reached the Hooker and exploded into a net, coruscating filaments of light shooting out and wrapping themselves around the demon. For the first time, Blowe saw every detail of the Hooker: the empty eye sockets, the grey, hanging skin, the tattered cloak of hatred and bitterness and jealousy hanging off its emaciated body. Then the net of light drew in, tighter and tighter, the scream getting higher and thinner until the light pulled into a tiny orb, a brilliant star which winked out, puffing black, greasy smoke into the air, which also then disappeared. Something fell to the ground with a *clink*.

Suzanna turned to Blowe and flinched, no doubt at the look of deep suspicion he was giving her. He stared at her, trying to see only one of her. The pain from his hands had gone, but his vision was failing, alternating between tunnelled darkness and scattered stars in every hue.

This is what happens when you attack demons, he thought. He couldn't tell if she looked normal now, instead of a woman-shaped patch of darkness, or if he was hallucinating.

"What are you?" he slurred, before slumping to the pavement.

***

The new office was small, but it was his, and it had a telephone and room for a desk and a filing cabinet. That was really all he needed in terms of space. There was even room for another chair in front of the desk, as well as one behind it, which was a plus because people liked to sit down while explaining their woes.

He looked at the door. Frosted glass blurred the lettering, but he knew what it said.

ROBERT BLOWE, PRIVATE INVESTIGATOR

He liked the font, with its slight fussiness. It reminded him that he was prepared to do unreasonable things in order to be at ease with himself. Never again would he have to let a case go because the CPS wanted to do a deal. He could choose which cases to take and how far he took them. And follow them to the bitter end, if necessary.

He looked out the window. The sun was shining and he had no clients yet. Might as well take advantage of the quiet while he could. He didn't anticipate being run off his feet, but he had a suspicion that there were some cases no one else would touch. Men made of swirling shadows killing people, tiny balls of light, people disappearing and reappearing with no memory of where they'd been...

There was a niche there, for someone with his abilities.

He went down the stairs and paused in the doorway. It was a commercial street. The kebab shop underneath him wouldn't open until late afternoon, which was handy, as their business hours would only overlap a little. He stepped onto the pavement, turned right, and stopped.

Sitting on the step outside the kebab shop was a thin, wiry figure with tousled black hair. David looked up at Blowe apologetically.

"I'm not dealin' no more," he said.

"That's… good."

"I heard you weren't a cop no more, neither."

"That's right." Blowe was surprised at how little that hurt. When he finished training he'd thought he'd be a cop to the end of his days — an end which he'd known even then would most likely occur on the street, on the wrong end of a bullet, but whatever. He'd been so sure of his path.

"They said you was a PI now."

Blowe nodded.

Silence. David's Adam's apple bobbed.

"I was wonderin' if maybe PIs ever need, like, an assistant. Someone to run about an' stuff. Take messages an' that."

Blowe considered this for a moment.

"I have a telephone for that," he pointed out mildly.

"Yeah, but maybe sometimes you need to talk to people what doesn't 'ave a phone."

"Are you asking me for a job, David? Because I only just set up and I don't even have any clients yet."

"I'm askin' if you need 'elp. An' you'll 'ave clients. People what sees stuff. Like you and I saw stuff."

Blowe felt his eyebrows climb.

"You saw it, too?" He hadn't realised. Shame swept over him. The kid must have been terrified. "What did you do after I passed out?"

David looked at his hands.

"When I realised you wasn't be'ind me, I come back for you. An' I saw that woman pick you up. I was gonna say summink, but she just looked at me an'… well… I fol'owed 'er, though. She took you 'ome. I figured you'd be alright, cos if she was gonna 'urt you, she coulda done it on the street, right there. And she coulda hurt me too, cos she knew I was followin', but she didn't. So I thought you was alright, and I left."

At least now he knew how he'd ended up in his own bed.

"I appreciate your concern. I'm sorry I couldn't do more to help."

"S'alright. You did what 'ad to be done. You tried to help Doyle." David shook his head, stood up, and dusted himself off. "I don't deal no more, Mr. Blowe. But I need to eat, y'know? So, I was finking, if you need any 'elp, I could do it. And I could be useful in uvver ways, Mr. Blowe."

Blowe looked around at the sunny street. Shops were open and the odd person wandered in and out of various places, mostly elderly ladies with their shopping bags on wheels, getting in ahead of the rush. Some mothers with a child or two, with or without pushchair.

None of them knew what could be hiding in the shadows. Because none of them could see it. Except maybe really young kids, who he'd often seen react to things he could see but their parents couldn't. That was probably the scariest thought of all. He nodded slowly to himself, then dug a hand in his pocket.

"Here," he said, grabbing David's hand and dumping a half-handful of change into it. "Go and get us some doughnuts, will you? Well, some doughnuts for me, and whatever you fancy. Might as well live up to at least one cliché."

David grinned so wide Blowe wondered if his face might freeze like that, and then decided it wouldn't be the worst thing. Better than a mask of terror.

"Doughnuts works for me. I'll be back in a tick." And he loped off up the street, waving hello to Mr. Tilman who was fiddling with something outside his hardware shop.

The click of high heels reached Blowe just before a familiar scent.

"Detective Blowe, still saving the world."

Blowe turned slowly, trying to keep his face relaxed.

"Actually it's Mr. Blowe, now." He was impressed. His voice barely trembled at all.

"So I heard," said Suzanna. "May I speak with you?"

He glanced at the open door leading up the stairs to his new office — his new world.

"Ah, what the hell." He stood aside and indicated the stairway. "Ladies first."

"I'm flattered, Mr. Blowe," she told him as she went ahead of him, her hips swaying just below his line of sight as she climbed the stairs. For some reason he wasn't finding his thoughts clouded, or that scent of hers overwhelming. She was just... an incredibly hot woman voluntarily entering his place of work.

He sighed. Nothing good would come of this.

Suzanna sat in the chair in front of the desk and watched him go around to sit on the other side.

"Do you have a problem, Suzanna?"

She smiled, perfect white teeth gleaming. He couldn't help checking for fangs. Then he remembered.

"Of course! I'm so sorry, I totally forgot about your friend—"

Suzanna waved a hand.

"I have no friends."

"But, in the park, you said..."

"I knew the Hooker would seek you out." She shrugged. "As you may remember, they would prefer not to go through me."

"You were... protecting me," Blowe said slowly. "That barbecue...?"

"A useful cover for such a disgusting smelling creature."

Blowe nodded, his stomach turning over. He'd barely thought twice when he saw those students. The Hooker could have taken him so easily.

"Thank you. That's twice now."

She raised an eyebrow.

"That you've saved my life." He blew out a breath. "It's a good thing I don't have an ego problem. A man could end up feeling inadequate."

She smiled.

"You killed the creature in the end. They were right. More's the pity."

"Who was right? And why is that a pity?"

"You are a fine looking man, Mr. Blowe. So tall, and strong, and clear of heart—" Her eyes started glowing, but she winced and broke off, and the colour faded.

"You fed from me?" Blowe was horrified, and part of it was because he was also a bit flattered.

"I only took a tiny, tiny bit! A girl has to feed! But fine, I will not eat your precious pet."

"Wha—?"

She glowered at him and tapped the jewel in her forehead.

"Like I said, you are important. I must protect you. It is a particularly cruel punishment."

"What for?" Blowe was intrigued. "And who by?"

Suzanna waved a hand languidly.

"That... is not important. All you need concern yourself with is that I am here, for your protection."

"But I've got this." Blowe lifted the edge of his jacket to draw her attention to the Glock of Destiny nestled under his arm. "I don't need your protection."

"Mr. Blowe," she said, her eyes full of pity, "there are more evils in this world than Hookers. You know this. That cannot protect you from everything. It is not infallible."

Blowe felt the Glock turn heavy in its holster and balled his hands into fists to keep from pulling it out and shooting her.

"It has a mind of its own, you see," Suzanna murmured. "A thirsty tool. Understandable. After all, it has tasted the blood of gods."

Blowe frowned.

"I thought... just one god."

That eyebrow arched again.

"Very well, Mr. I Only Just Found Out Demons And Angels Are Real. You know best."

"Angels?"

"Of course. Why do you think you are able to wield the weapon?"

"Wha—? But..."

"Relax. You are only a very, *very* small part angel. Do not get too excited."

He glowered at her, but was distracted by footsteps pounding up the stairs. David lurched through the doorway with a large doughnut box in his hands.

"Your change," he said, holding out a closed fist towards Blowe.

Doughnuts *and* change? Maybe this would work out after all.

Then David saw Suzanna.

"Er, hi."

"Hello." She gave him a white-hot smile and Blowe rolled his eyes. *And maybe not.*

"She's a succubus," he said to David, then reached out and gave him back the change. "Here's your first pay."

David rolled his eyes, but started counting the coins with a smile he couldn't quite hide.

Turning his attention to Suzanna, Blowe added, "You can't eat him either."

She rolled her eyes.

"I fed last night, if you recall. I will not need to feed for several more days."

"Yeah," said Blowe. "I recall."

David opened the doughnut box and offered it to Suzanna, trying to lean away without making it look too obvious.

"Ladies first."

She licked her lips.

"I really shouldn't. Sugar dampens my, er..."

"Take two," Blowe suggested.

David looked at the phone.

"Mr. Blowe, your phone—"

It started to ring. He glared at it, his shoulders slumping.

"It's about to ring."

Suzanna took a delicate bite of a doughnut. Her eyes immediately rolled back in her head. Blowe considered David.

"You can help in other ways, eh?"

The kid looked sheepish.

"Is it safe to answer that?" Blowe asked.

"Oh, yeah, I just..." He shrugged and took another bite. Jam exploded across his face. Blowe made a grab for a doughnut before they all vanished and picked up the phone.

"Blowe."

Thank You

I'm so glad you decided to pick up this story and I hope you enjoyed it. If you did (or even if you didn't!) please consider writing a review, or even just telling your friends, so that they can benefit too.

Also, if you enjoyed the story and would like to read more of my work, you can find a list of my published work on my website, **www.mhairisimpson.com**. You can also sign up there for my new releases mailing list if you'd like to be among the first to know when I'm going to have a new release out. It's strictly for telling you about upcoming releases and giving you the option to get the newest story before anyone else.

If you'd like to contact me, please do! You can email me at **mhairi@mhairisimpson.com**. I look forward to hearing from you!

Acknowledgements

I'm so glad this story is getting let out into the wild again, after a period in mourning for the demise of its former home, Anachron Press. Colin Barnes called my bluff and this tale is the result. His excellent editing took a very ropey first draft and made it a story. Kait, Ren and Leona have always been there for me, most of all when most sane people would stay away! And Adele, Susan, Kait, Amanda and Caroline are just the perfect enablers - I'd follow my dreams regardless but maybe not with so much laughter and grinning! Lastly special thanks should go to Alasdair Stuart, whose effervescent review of Hookers in its first incarnation was almost as long as the story itself. I love you guys - thank you.

About The Author

Mhairi Simpson is a fantasy writer (mostly blood and inner demons) and inveterate traveller (mostly Europe and South America). An only child who grew up in boarding schools and with a background in modern languages and paper pushing, Mhairi has spent most of her life with words on a page, leading her to realise her best shot at faking sanity is to be a full time author/editor. She is most effectively bribed/tamed/friended with chocolate.

Find her online at:
Her website, Reality Refugee: http://mhairisimpson.com
Twitter: http://twitter.com/AMhairiSimpson
Facebook:
http://www.facebook.com/MhairiSimpsonAuthor